# The Fairy Tinker And The Tiny Ghost
## Spooky The Tiny Ghost Went Missing

Author: John L. Brown
Illustrated: By: John L. Brown
Copyright © 2021 By: John L. Brown

Hi, my name is Tinker and I'm a magical fairy that sprinkles magic everywhere I go. My dad called me tinker stinker when I was much younger. I'm out in front of the castle sprinkling magic on the flowers with my little friend, Spooky the tiny ghost.

As I finished sprinkling magic on the beautiful flowers, I turned around and noticed that Spooky was gone, and a bird with funny legs was standing where I had last seen Spooky. The bird told me that Spooky was gone and I needed to search for him.

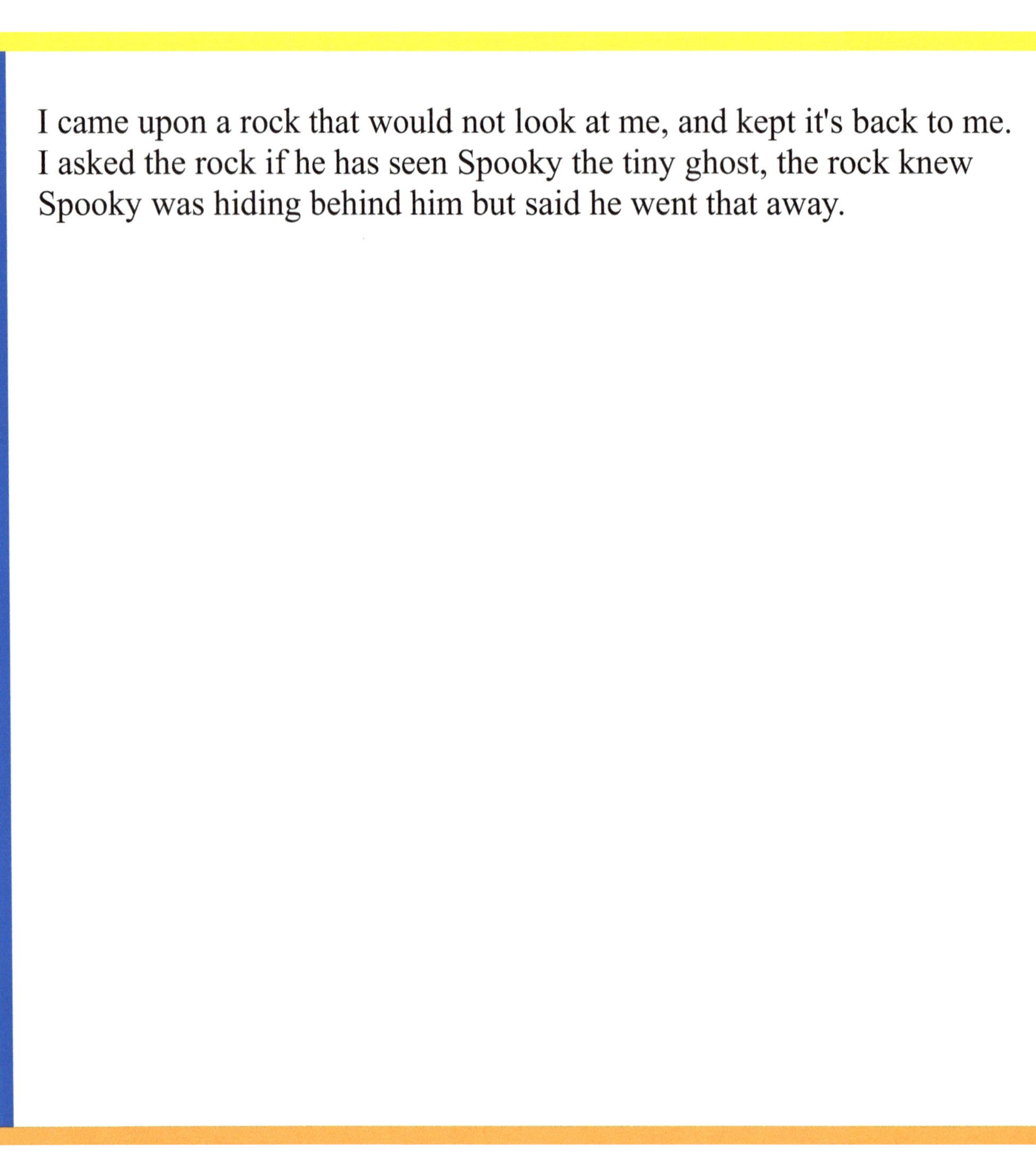

I came upon a rock that would not look at me, and kept it's back to me.
I asked the rock if he has seen Spooky the tiny ghost, the rock knew
Spooky was hiding behind him but said he went that away.

I saw a crooked house in the distance and flew down to check it out. There were two funny looking snakes staring at each other, so I asked them if they have seen Spooky the tiny ghost, and the yellow one laughed and said, you'll have to keep searching.

I came upon a girl reading a book and I asked her about Spooky the tiny ghost and she did not answer me, so I asked again, still no answer, when I asked for a third time she said, I'm sorry, I'm reading my book and I will talk to you when I'm finished. I sprinkled some magic and left.

I saw a beautiful garden of colorful flowers and went down to spread some magic, when I saw a flying saucer flying near me. I asked the alien inside and he took off as if he never saw a fairy flying before.

I was looking down at this strange place and saw strange looking characters. I got closer and asked if anyone has seen Spooky the tiny ghost. No one answered me and kept waving at something, so I spread some magic and went on.

I thought I had seen it all until I saw a pink rabbit sitting on a flying lamb, a smiling sun, a blue bird flying, and three baby birds in a nest on the ground. The animals here seem to be crazy, so I got out of there.

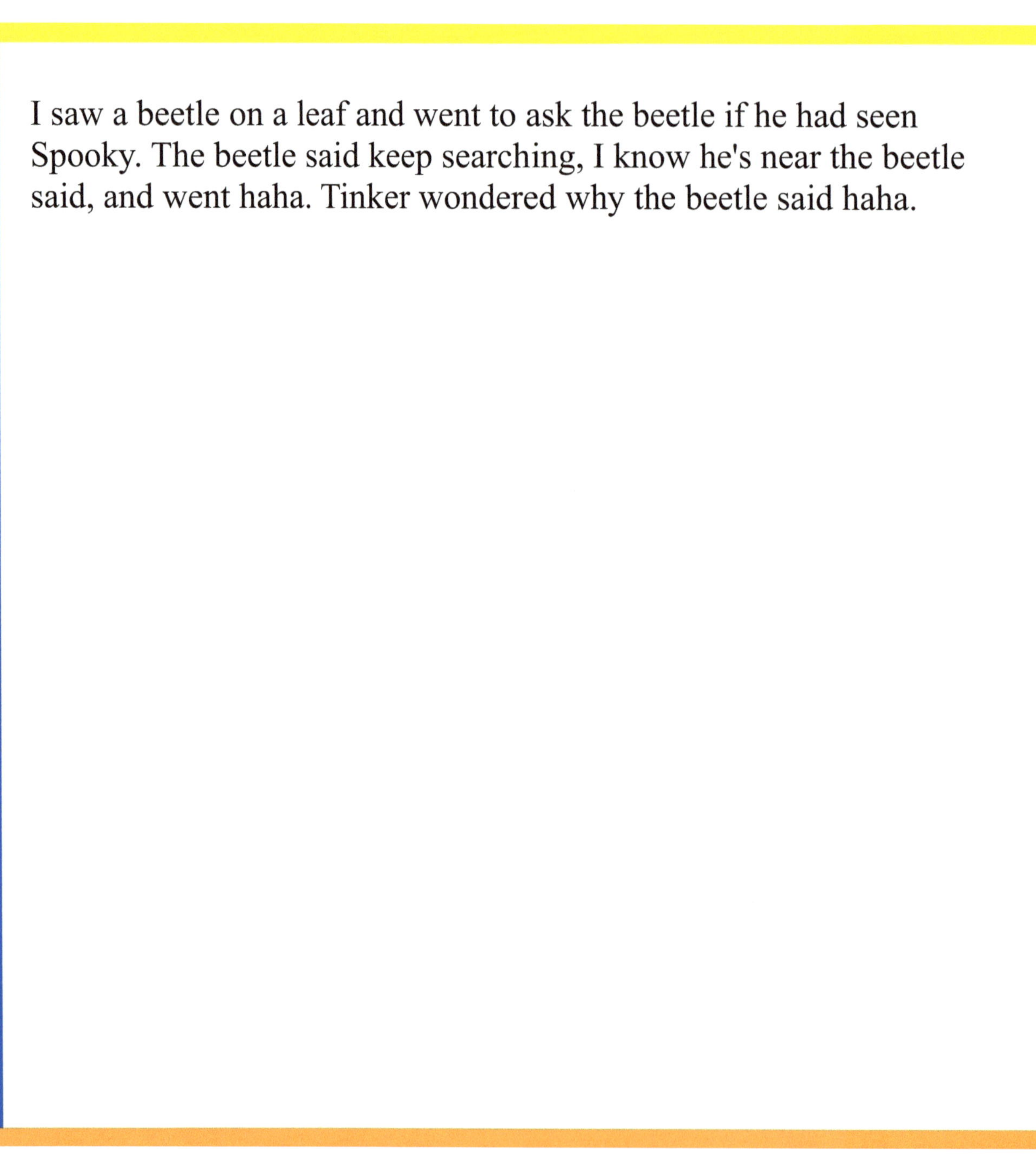

I saw a beetle on a leaf and went to ask the beetle if he had seen Spooky. The beetle said keep searching, I know he's near the beetle said, and went haha. Tinker wondered why the beetle said haha.

I came to a girl leaning on a fence. It looked like she was dreaming or hoping for something. I said, little girl, do you know where Spooky the tiny ghost is? No, the little girl replies, and said, I know he's near while laughing.

Tinker was starting to think that, everyone she has talked to knows more then they're saying because some of them were laughing as I left. I wonder if Spooky is behind this?

Wow a girl riding a large turtle. Hey little girl, have you seen my friend Spooky the tiny ghost. No, the little girl replies and said, he is closer than you think, and rode off with her turtle, smiling.

Tinker was sprinkling some magic on a butterfly when she saw an alligator standing upright with a flower, how strange Tinker thought to herself. Have you seen Spooky the tiny ghost? Why no he's not in my garden the alligator replied, giggling.

I came upon this strange forest with perfectly formed leaves on the trees. I saw a little dog that I woke up and the dog said, no I haven't seen Spooky and went back to sleep. Tinker said, I didn't even ask the dog anything.

I saw a man playing with his dog and flew down and asked him if he had seen a tiny little ghost? The man answered and said, I thought I saw something a minute ago, but a little girl came by a while ago searching for something too. She went that way. Tinker went in that direction.

I found the little girl and she told me that Spooky had been hiding from you all of this time. Spooky had all of his friends in on this and none of them would tell you. If you go back to the castle, you'll find Spooky waiting there for you. Tinker was furious and said this is not funny, and flew off.

When I returned to the castle, there was Spooky and some friends and they were laughing up a storm. I yelled at Spooky and told him, it was not funny, but forgave him because I was just happy he was alright.

I will always spread magic to all with love. Bye now from Tinker and Spooky.